My Heaven Book

2021 Third Printing
2017 Second Printing
2016 First Printing

My Heaven Book

Copyright © 2016 by Paraclete Press

ISBN 978-1-61261-643-8

Acknowledgments:
"There'll be no sorrow there" text by Lewis Hartsough, 1858.
"Jesus Loves Me" text by Anna B. Warner.

Library of Congress Cataloging-in-Publication Data
Names: Simpson, Clare, author. | Angelina, Maria, illustrator.
Title: My heaven book / author, Clare Simpson ; illustrator, Maria Angelina.
Description: Brewster MA : Paraclete Press Inc., 2016.
Identifiers: LCCN 2015042732 | ISBN 9781612616438
Subjects: LCSH: Heaven–Christianity–Juvenile literature.
Classification: LCC BT849 .S56 2016 | DDC 236/.24–dc23
LC record available at http://lccn.loc.gov/2015042732

Published by Paraclete Press
Brewster, Massachusetts
www.paracletepress.com

Manufactured by RR Donnelley, Humen Dongguan.
Daning Village, Humen Town, Dongguan City,Guangdong 523930,PRC
Printed in July 2021. Dongguan, China

My Heaven
Book

Clare Simpson

ILLUSTRATED BY
Maria Angelina

PARACLETE PRESS
BREWSTER, MASSACHUSETTS

Tell Me About Heaven

Heaven is where God lives.
God wants all his children
to live there forever!

Heaven is a beautiful place
God planned for us.
It is more wonderful
than any of us can imagine.

I am a child of God
and God loves me.
Someday God will want me
to live in heaven
with him forever.

Jesus told a story about a tiny seed, called a mustard seed.

When it is planted it grows
so big that it becomes a tree and
all the birds can make their nests
in its branches.
That's what heaven is like.

From Matthew 13:31–32

9

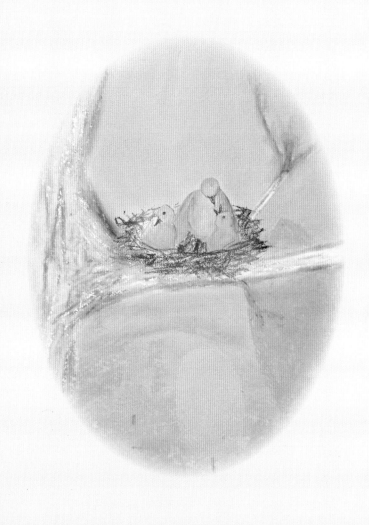

PRAYER

Now I lay me down to rest.

Angels guard my little nest.

Like a love bird in a tree,

heavenly Father, care for me.

Amen.

Does Heaven Have a Special Place for Me?

There is a lot of room

in heaven for you.

Jesus tells us that heaven
is his Father's house.
It has many rooms.

Jesus is getting one ready

just for you to live in someday.

From John 14:2–3

Heaven is not a crying place!

Heaven is a rejoicing place!

17

We go to heaven

when we need it most.

BLESSING

Surely goodness and mercy
shall follow me all the days of my life,
and I shall dwell in the house of
the Lord forever.

From Psalm 23:6 RSV

How Do I Get to Heaven?

I hear about heaven, but where is it found?

Can anyone get there? Who is heaven bound?

I know that I want to see heaven someday

and live there forever, I hope and I pray.

God loved the whole world so much
that he sent his own Son here,
and gave him to us,

so that if we believe in him we won't die but will live forever in heaven.

From John 3:16

25

Jesus loves me! He who died,

Heaven's gate to open wide.

He will wash away my sin,

let his little child come in.

Anna B. Warner

PRAYER

I pray each night and ask the Lord above,

to stay with me in his mercy and his love.

Keep me safe from all earthly harm,

and someday bring me

into your gentle arms.

Amen.

29

Who Made Heaven?

In the beginning God made heaven and earth,

and he saw that they were very good.

From Genesis 1:1, 1:31

God made everything we can see

and everything we cannot see.

If we think that earth is a good place to live,

just imagine how special heaven will be!

36

When I look up into the heavens,
I see the stars and the moon.
I know you made them all.
I feel so small,
but I know you love me.

From Psalm 8:3–4

37

I love to sing of Heaven,

Where white-robed angels are;

Where many friends are gathered safe

From fear, and pain, and care.

There'll be no sorrow there,

There'll be no sorrow there;

In heaven above, where all is love,

There'll be no sorrow there.

Lewis Hartsough, 1858

PRAYER

Our Father who is in heaven,

your name is holy.

Your kingdom come, your will be done,

here on earth as it already is in heaven. *Amen.*

From Matthew 6:9–10

Will I See Jesus in Heaven?

While Jesus was blessing his friends,

he left them and was taken up into heaven.

Luke 24:51 NIV

Jesus taught us a lot about heaven,

and he is your special friend.

If you ask him, he will stay in your heart

now, and some joyful day you will see him

in heaven.

Jesus told another story about how important heaven is. He said it was like a treasure that a man found in a field. The man was so excited that he sold everything else he had, and went and bought that field.

From Matthew 13:44

You are Jesus's treasure.

PRAYER

Be near me Lord Jesus; I ask you to stay

close by me forever and love me, I pray.

Bless all the dear children

in your tender care, and fit us for heaven

to live with you there. Amen.

Traditional